SIMON & SCHUSTER BOOKS FOR YOUNG READERS
An imprint of Simon & Schuster Children's Publishing Division
1230 Avenue of the Americas, New York, New York 10020
Copyright © 2020 by Nicola Killen
Originally published in Great Britain in 2020 by Simon & Schuster UK Ltd
All rights reserved, including the right of reproduction in whole or in part in any form.
SIMON & SCHUSTER BOOKS FOR YOUNG READERS is a trademark of Simon & Schuster, Inc.
For information about special discounts for bulk purchases, please contact Simon & Schuster
Special Sales at 1-866-506-1949 or business@simonandschuster.com.
The Simon & Schuster Speakers Bureau can bring authors to your live event.
For more information or to book an event, contact the Simon & Schuster Speakers
Bureau at 1-866-248-3049 or visit our website at www.simonspeakers.com.
Book design by Tom Daly
The text for this book was set in Corda.
Manufactured in China
1219 SUK
First Edition
10 9 8 7 6 5 4 3 2 1
CIP data for this book is available from the Library of Congress
ISBN 978-1-5344-6696-8
ISBN 978-1-5344-6697-5 (eBook)

THE
LITTLE KITTEN

Nicola Killen

A Paula Wiseman Book
Simon & Schuster Books for Young Readers
New York   London   Toronto   Sydney   New Delhi

It was a crisp autumn morning and Ollie was heading outside to play, closely followed by her cat, Pumpkin.

Meow!

Ollie was about to jump
into a pile of leaves when
she noticed it was moving!

She tried to take a closer look
but suddenly the wind whistled,

blowing the leaves
EVERYWHERE.

Hiding underneath was a little shivering kitten.

Ollie scooped the kitten into her arms and cuddled him until he felt warm.

The little kitten was very friendly and soon the three of them were playing together.

They started with a game of hide-and-seek,

"One … two … three … four … five …"

before catching falling leaves

and being explorers!

After so much excitement,
it was time for a rest.

But it wasn't long until the little kitten wanted to play again!

Ollie was having so much fun, she forgot about Pumpkin napping under the tree . . .

and ran farther and
farther into the woods.

When the new friends reached the heart of the woods,
Ollie noticed there were posters everywhere.
She looked closer and saw a familiar face staring back.

It was the kitten and someone was looking for him!

"I need to take you home," Ollie whispered. "Do you know where that is?"

The kitten meowed and suddenly the wind whistled, whipping hundreds of leaves into the air.

As the leaves settled, they revealed a secret path.

The kitten set off right away,
with Ollie close behind.

Where would it lead them?

It was the kitten's home!

Ollie waved good-bye. She felt sad but knew the kitten had someone who loved him just as much as she loved ... Pumpkin!

"Oh, Pumpkin," sobbed Ollie as she realized she'd left her own cat behind.

She hurried back through the
woods, unsure of the way,

not noticing the sky getting
darker and darker.

Lost and alone, Ollie sat down.

As a tear trickled down her cheek,
she heard a rustle in the leaves . . .

. . . and a familiar **meow!**

"Pumpkin! You found me!
I'm so sorry I left you behind."

Purring loudly, Ollie's cat led
her out of the woods

and toward home.

That night, Ollie wasn't the only one
happy to be reunited with her cat.

And in the morning, Ollie opened the door
to find a very special thank-you gift!